Meet The Author –  KU-766-384

What is your favourite animal?
Elephant
What is your favourite boy's name?
David
What is your favourite girl's name?
Sarah
What is your favourite food?
Prawns
What is your favourite music?
Dean Martin singing
That's Amore
What is your favourite hobby?
Writing

Meet The Illustrator – Karen Donnelly

What is your favourite animal?
Woodlice!
What is your favourite boy's name?
Laurie
What is your favourite girl's name?
Jean
What is your favourite food?
Sausages and runny eggs
What is your favourite music?
Beck
What is your favourite hobby?
Drawing and printmaking

To the Spateston Boys –
Mark, Greg, Duncan, Dean and Ross

Contents

Chapter 1
Markie and Me

This is how it all began. One day Markie and me were playing football in the park after school.

Well, Markie was playing football. I was in goal, leaning against the posts. Markie was playing with the ball. He was showing off to the girls who were standing at the side watching him.

Girls always watch Markie. He's the best looking boy in the school. At least, that's what he says. I'm Duncan and Markie's my best pal. Him and I are what you call "cool". We dress cool. We act cool. We are cool.

We weren't in the football team. We weren't in a gang. Lots of people wanted to be our friends, but Markie and me didn't need anyone else. Some people in the school didn't even like us! They thought we were show-offs. We weren't show-offs. We were just better than everyone else.

Anyway, Markie was bouncing the ball off his head when I heard barking from across the park. I looked over and saw Ross. He was trying to hold back some of his dogs on leads. They were pulling away from him and they looked really scared. They were jumping about and yelping. Ross kept tripping over as he tried to hold them back.

Ross came from this odd family who were always taking in stray dogs. I can't

tell you how many they had. Their house must have been an awful mess.

Ross looked like a stray himself. His bright, woolly jumpers were too big for him. His dark hair stood up like a toilet brush.

Ross would have liked to be our friend. He waved at us every day when he came to the park. But Ross? A friend of ours? Come on. Get real.

What was the matter with those dogs? Every day, when they came into the park, they seemed really scared of something. I knew what they'd do next. They'd race off and drag Ross round the park on his belly.

It was great fun to watch.

I was so busy looking at Ross that I didn't see what Markie was doing. He had stopped bouncing the ball on his head and had kicked it towards the goal. I turned and saw the ball racing at me.

"Duncan!" Markie yelled at me. It was too late. The ball slammed into my face and everything went black.

When I came round, Markie was bending over me. "Are you all right?" he said. "Duncan, pal, speak to me!"

I blinked and tried to focus my eyes.

Then the girls came rushing up to us. "Did you hurt yourself?" They sounded worried.

I was just about to reply when I saw that they weren't talking to me. They were talking to Markie.

"I'm the one who was hit!" I told them as Markie helped me to stand up. They didn't care about me. They stood round Markie like a fan club. They wanted to be sure that he hadn't hurt his foot when he kicked the ball.

I could still hear those dogs yelping. I looked over at them.

No wonder they were yelping. A tall, lanky boy with red hair was kicking them. That made me mad. I hate to see animals getting hurt. I ran across to him. "You leave those dogs alone!" I yelled.

Ross looked up at me. "Me? I've not been near them."

"Not you. *Him*!" I pointed at the boy with red hair. I saw now that his clothes were odd. He wore a long, black jacket and tight, black trousers. His black shoes had long, pointed toes. Wow! I would hate to be kicked by him. His hair was swept up like a tidal wave.

He looked amazed. "Can you see me?"

"Of course I can see you," I said. "If you kick those dogs one more time, you'll be sorry."

Ross looked at me as if he was going to cry. "Me? I'd never kick my dogs."

"Not you, Ross. *Him!*"

I pointed again at the boy with the red hair. He stuck his tongue out at me. "Make me stop!" he said and he kicked the dogs again.

That was it! I flung myself at the boy.

And that's when the most amazing thing happened.

I went right through him.

The dogs rushed off across the park, dragging Ross behind them.

I landed on the grass and yelled, "How did I do that?"

The boy with the red hair was jumping about like a wild man. "Brilliant!" he yelled. "You can see me. No-one's ever been able to see me before."

"See you?" I said. "What do you mean?"

"Are you thick?" He bent down over me. The smell was awful. And I saw now that he had one blue eye and one green eye. I was beginning to feel really bad about what was going on.

"I'm a ghost," he said softly.

Chapter 2
Spooked

I think I blacked out again. When I opened my eyes Markie was slapping my face.

"Are you OK, pal?" he said.

"I had an awful dream, Markie," I said. I began to tell him, but then I saw the tall boy with the red hair, black jacket and pointed shoes. He was standing near

Markie and he was grinning in a very nasty way.

"Can you see him, Markie?" I pointed at the boy. He was so close I could almost touch his face.

Markie looked round. "Who? Do you mean Ross?" He began to laugh, because there was Ross, still being dragged round the park on his belly.

"Not Ross, no – *him*!"

Markie looked to see where my finger was pointing. He was staring right into the boy's face. The boy stuck out his tongue. I waited for Markie to punch him. He wasn't going to let the boy get away with that.

But Markie looked back at me and said, "No-one there, pal." Then he sniffed. "But there's an awful smell. Is it you?"

The boy began to jump up and down. "No-one else can see me! No-one else can see me!" He was yelling with joy. "This is going to be fun. I've never haunted a person before."

I grabbed Markie's arm. "You've got to be able to see that boy," I said. "If you can't, it means he really is a …"

But how could he be a … *ghost*? He was as solid as me and Markie. He looked just like a normal boy, except for a green glow all around him – and that smell.

"He's a what?" Markie asked.

It was hard to get the words out. "He's a ghost."

"I am a ghost!" the boy yelled. "And my name's Dean. If I'm going to haunt you, you should at least know my name."

"He says his name's Dean. And he's going to haunt me."

Markie looked worried. "It was that bump on the head from the football. That's why you're seeing things. I'm going to take you home."

"I'm coming too," Dean said.

"NO!" I yelled and Markie looked upset.

"I'm only trying to help you, Duncan."

"I'm not talking to you!" I shouted at Markie. "I'm talking to him."

If there's one thing about Markie, it's this. He's the best friend you could ever have. At least, that's what he says.

"If you say there's a ghost there, there *is* a ghost there. You would never lie to me."

Markie stood up. "Right. Where is he? I'm going to sort him out."

He was ready for a fight and Markie is the best fighter in the school. At least, that's what he says. But I've never seen him fight with anyone. He just makes them laugh and that's it.

Markie held up his fists and began to jump about like a boxer. "Now, tell me where this ghost is. I'm going to punch him."

Poor Markie didn't have a hope of winning this one. I watched in horror as Dean breathed in, then blew out so hard that Markie was lifted off his feet and thrown across the park.

I jumped to my feet. "You're evil," I yelled at Dean.

Dean made a stupid face. "I'm a ghost. You think I'm going to be nice?"

I ran over to Markie. He was lying in a bush. He had mud all over him.

"Was that the ghost?" he asked.

"Yes, it was," I said.

Markie looked around. "Is he still here?"

He was there all right, standing behind Markie.

Markie sniffed. The smell was awful, like rotting fish. "I think I can smell him."

Dean didn't like that one bit. He kicked Markie on the shin. Then he sat down on the grass and stared at his pointed shoes.

"Hope that kick hasn't done my winkle-pickers any harm," he said. "They're cool, aren't they?"

I thought his pointed shoes looked stupid, but I didn't say that.

Markie was jumping about, holding his shin. "I thought ghosts couldn't hurt you?"

"I can," Dean said. "I can kick and punch and no-one can see me. It's fun being a ghost."

"Remember I can see you now," I told him.

"I know. And that's going to be fun too. You're never going to get rid of me, Duncan," said Dean.

Chapter 3
Dead Funny

Markie phoned me that night. "Is the ghost still there?"

"He's still here," I said. In fact, Dean was sitting on my bed. The smell was awful. "My mum's not happy at all. She says something smells funny."

"Of course I smell funny," Dean said. "I've been dead for about 50 years."

I took no notice.

I pulled the duvet over my head and spoke softly into the phone to Markie, "My mum thinks I've got a dead cat in here. And the ghost's making an awful mess."

He was too. He had thrown my games everywhere. He had pulled my clothes out of my drawers and scattered them round the room. "Mum's going to kill me when she sees what he's done."

"I'm coming to see you," Markie told me.

He soon arrived. As he stepped into the room, Dean tripped him up. Markie landed in a pile of my dirty washing.

"Where is he?" yelled Markie. "I'm going to get him this time."

Markie had jumped up and was turning this way and that. So was Dean. One moment he was in front of Markie, punching his nose, and the next he was behind him, kicking him in the backside.

Dean thought it was dead funny.

"But I came here with a plan to help him," Markie cried.

"What's your plan?" Dean and I said at the same time.

"It's a great plan," Markie said.

It had to be a great plan. Markie is the smartest boy in school. At least that's what he says.

"We're going to help him to rest in peace," Markie said.

"How?" Dean and I asked at the same time.

"How did Dean die? Ask him if it was murder. Does he want us to find who did it and get him put in prison?"

Dean shook his head. "It wasn't murder."

I told this to Markie.

"Maybe there was something he wanted to do before he died that he wants us to do for him," Markie said. "Did he want to tell someone that he loved them, or something like that?"

"What a stupid idea!" Dean laughed.

"He says that's a stupid idea," I told Markie.

"I'm only trying to help," Markie said. "How did he die anyway?"

Dean thought for a moment. "I can't remember. It was a long time ago."

"He can't remember how he died," I told Markie.

Markie couldn't believe this. "You couldn't forget something like that," he said.

Dean was trying to think. "I remember I had a firework in my hand, and I was chasing a dog with it. That dog was really scared. I was having such a laugh! That's the last thing I remember."

When I told Markie what Dean had said, Markie went mad! "If that's why he's a ghost," he said, "I don't even know why we're trying to help him."

Dean came up very close to Markie and blew at him. Markie's face went green. I thought he was going to faint. "That ghost stinks," he said.

Dean blew Markie right off the bed. Then he turned to me and said, "You tell your pal, Markie, that I don't want any help. I like being a ghost. It's even better fun now someone can see me."

When I told Markie this he stood up. "OK, Duncan, that's it," he said. "We're going to get rid of that ghost."

Dean couldn't stop laughing. "Over my dead body!" he said, and laughed so much *he* fell off the bed. "Get the joke? Over my dead body!"

Chapter 4

Help! I'm Stuck with a Ghost!

Dean was still sitting on my bed when I woke up next morning. He still smelt awful.

"What *is* that smell, Duncan?" my mum asked me at breakfast. "Is it your feet?"

That made Dean laugh so much he pulled the cloth off the table. The plates and cups crashed onto the floor.

I got the blame for that too.

"We've got to get this ghost to go," I told Markie when I met him at the school gates.

"Is he with you now?" asked Markie.

I'll never hear the end of this

In reply, Dean tripped him up, and Markie fell flat on his face in a puddle. Someone behind us was laughing at him.

"Look at the cool guy!" It was Sunna, the only girl in the school who didn't fancy Markie. "Not so cool now, are you, Markie?"

Markie frowned at her. I think he fancies Sunna but of course he'd never say that. I helped him to get up. He nodded. "We've just got to get that ghost to go!" he said.

Sunna went off laughing.

"She doesn't like Markie much, does she?" Dean was pleased about that. His one green eye and his one blue eye had a wicked glint in them. "I could make her like him even less." And he stuck out his foot and tripped her up. Now she was the one who went face down in a puddle.

She was back on her feet at once. She was very angry. She looked right at Markie.

"It wasn't me!" he yelled at her. But she didn't believe him. She ran at him, swung him round three times and sent him spinning into the bushes.

Markie had never looked so uncool.

He was in a very bad mood when we went into class. Everyone had seen what Sunna had done and they were all laughing at him. Me and Markie aren't used to that. And it was all Dean's fault. He was sitting beside me, grinning.

I don't understand why no-one could see him. He looked as solid as you and me. But he did have this green glow around him ... and the smell. Everyone was moving away from me and sniffing.

"You smell disgusting," Sunna said in a loud voice.

Mr Barr, our teacher, looked up. He was sniffing too. "Have you got a dead dog in your bag, Duncan?" he asked. And he laughed until his wig wobbled.

"Did he say I smelt like a dead dog?" Dean asked.

"You do smell like a dead dog," I told him.

It was my bad luck that Mr Barr thought I was saying it to him.

"Come here, Duncan!" he said. I came up to his desk with Dean just behind me.

"You do smell awful, boy!" Mr Barr said and he held his nose.

That made Dean mad. "I'm going to make him sorry he said that," he told me.

"Shut up!" I yelled. Dean was getting me into real trouble.

"What did you say?" said Mr Barr, getting more and more angry.

"I didn't mean you, sir," I told him.

Then, to my horror, Dean snatched Mr Barr's wig right off his head. I tried to stop him – and of course what did it look like? It looked as if I was the one who had taken off his wig.

Mr Barr was yelling at me. He had his hands over his bald head. The class was going crazy. Dean threw the wig across the room. It hit Markie in the face.

"So you two are in this together! Now you're both in real trouble!" said Mr Barr.

We were taken off to the Head's office. Dean danced after us. He was enjoying every moment.

"I love being a ghost!" Dean was yelling.

Markie and I just looked at each other.

"We've got to get that ghost to go!" we said.

Chapter 5
Enter Greg

The Head went on and on at us for ages. Dean made things worse by knocking all the papers off his desk. We got the blame for that. Then he spilt tea all down the Head's shirt. We got the blame for that too. It wasn't fair.

"Were you as awful as this when you were still alive?" Markie asked Dean as we walked home.

"Hey, look at the cool guys," Sunna shouted, so everyone could hear her. "They're talking to someone who's not there."

Everyone was laughing at me and Markie. Well, we're just not used to that.

Greg was the only one who didn't laugh. Greg's the school nerd. He'd rather read a book than go to the cinema. And he uses the computer to find out stuff for his school work, instead of playing games. He looks just like Harry Potter – dark, floppy hair and glasses. All he needs is the scar.

Greg was looking at us now. He walked across to me and Markie. "It seems to me that you and your friend are acting in a very odd manner," he said.

Greg always talks like that. No wonder he annoys everyone.

"There must be a reason why you two are acting so oddly," Greg went on. "And I ask myself what that reason could be. Would you like to tell me what's going on?"

My eyes lit up. I turned to Markie.

"Markie," I said, "this could be just what we need. Greg is really clever. He knows everything. He could help us ..." Then I went on too softly for Dean to hear, "... he could help us get this ghost to go."

Markie wasn't keen. "He's a nerd, Duncan. We can't be seen around with someone like Greg."

Dean came closer to Markie and me. "What are you two on about?" he hissed.

Greg came closer to us too. Too close. His face went green. "What's that awful smell?" he asked.

Dean sniffed under his arms. "It's not me that's smelly. And I don't like you saying it is." Then he hit Greg on the nose. Markie grabbed him just as he fell.

"Who did that?" Greg asked.

"You won't believe us," I said.

"Try me," said Greg.

Then we told him everything. We told him how I had first seen Dean just after my bump on the head. We told him that he was still there, but I was the only person who could see him. We told him Dean wanted to haunt me – for ever.

"It sounds as if the bump on the head made it possible for you to see ghosts. Things like that do happen," Greg said. He nodded his head very wisely. His nose was

still bleeding. "You say he dresses in a funny way?"

"Dresses funny!" That made Dean cross. "Let me tell you, everyone thinks I'm dead cool. I'm a teddy boy."

"He says he's a teddy boy," I told Greg.

Greg nodded. "I've heard of them," he said. "They wore tight, black trousers and long, pointed shoes called winkle-pickers. And they were 'cool' in their day. Myself, I always thought they looked stupid."

Dean's reply was to punch Greg on the nose again.

"I could help you get rid of him," Greg said, as he wiped more blood from his nose. He looked angry now.

"Do you think so?" Dean snarled as he kicked Greg on the ankle.

Greg yelped.

"He's driving us potty, Greg. So how are you going to help us get rid of him?"

"You'll never get rid of me," Dean said. "You're stuck with me for ever."

Then he grinned. That made him look really scary. His face went green and his teeth were blacker than ever.

Was I stuck with him for ever? What an awful idea. "Greg! You've got to help us. We've got to get that ghost to go!"

"All right," said Greg. "I'll help you. But only if you do something for me."

Chapter 6

From Worse, to
Even Worse!

Then Greg told us what he wanted and it
was not what we thought it would be. He
didn't want money. He didn't want Markie
to get him a girlfriend. He just wanted to
be cool. He told us he was fed up with being
a nerd. He wanted to be our friend. One of
our gang.

That was the hardest thing to do for him. Greg was the kind of guy we tried to stay away from. He wasn't normal. He did his homework. But we had no choice. So, we said he could be our friend and he said he would help us. He was going to find out all he could to help us get rid of Dean.

Dean was just behind me all the way home. He kicked a dog and it yelped and I got the blame. The owner was Mrs Todd who lived in our street, and she said she was going to phone my mum – so Dean kicked her too. Mrs Todd lifted me by the ear and dragged me home.

Was my mum mad!

"Kicking Mrs Todd's dog! And then kicking Mrs Todd! I'm ashamed of you, Duncan."

"But, Mum," I kept trying to explain. She wouldn't let me say a word. She only sniffed.

"And as for those feet, they stink. Get in a bath."

The bad thing was that Dean stayed in the bathroom with me the whole time. He sat on the toilet, and talked about how much he enjoyed being a ghost and how he would never leave me.

I phoned Markie.

"I'm going crazy. I don't care if Greg is a nerd. He can marry my sister if he helps us!"

"But think what all this will do for us, Duncan. If we let Greg be our friend we won't look cool anymore," Markie said.

"It's OK for you," I replied. "You don't have an ugly ghost sitting on your bed. No-one thinks you smell."

I knew Markie would help me. He was a true friend.

"OK, pal. I'll phone Greg and see if he's got a plan."

I put down the phone. Dean looked angry. "Did you call me ugly?" he said.

"Yeah, you are ugly. Look in the mirror."

Dean was so mad that he pulled out all my drawers, again, and threw all my clothes over the floor. I jumped off the bed and yelled, "Stop that!"

My mum came rushing into the room just as Dean was pushing all the books off the shelf and I was trying to stop him.

"What is wrong with you, Duncan? Why are you shouting like that? And look at this mess."

"It wasn't me, Mum," I tried to tell her. But why should she believe me? Who else could it be?

"You're telling me you've got someone I can't see in here?" she asked.

She held her nose. "And if that smell hasn't gone by the weekend, I'm taking you to the doctor. Even a *boy's* feet can't smell like that."

I lay down on the bed after she left me. Things were going from bad to worse.

Dean was sitting in a corner, laughing. I wasn't laughing at all. I knew then for sure. I'd got to get that ghost to go!

Chapter 7

We've Got to Get that Ghost to Go!

For the first time in my life I wanted to go to school. I didn't sleep at all that night, because Dean was sitting on my bed and he never stopped talking.

"Well, I've had no-one to talk to for years. Can you blame me?" he said.

I pulled the duvet over my head, but that awful smell was still there. It was like rotting fish, and it was getting worse every day.

"You look awful, Duncan," Markie said to me when he saw me at school.

I knew I did. I'd had a look in the mirror that morning. White face, black eyes and my hair standing on end. I looked more like a ghost than Dean did.

Greg came running over to us. "Hi, pals!" he shouted. I could see most of our class watching him. *Were Greg and Markie and me pals now? Something was wrong.*

"Have you got a plan?" I asked him.

"What plan?" Dean said.

Greg nodded. "We are going to get rid of him."

"Do you know how to do it?" we gasped.

"I went to the library last night and read every book I could about ghosts and why they haunt people. This one just seems to enjoy it." Greg looked proud of what he had done.

Dean laughed. "He's got that bit right," he said. "I do enjoy haunting people."

Greg went on talking, "And I read about how to get ghosts to go too. You have to EX-OR-CISE them. That's how you get rid of a ghost."

Markie jumped on Greg as if he'd just scored a goal. "You're brilliant, Greg!" he shouted.

I jumped on both of them. "What a guy!"

The whole school was looking at us now. But me and Markie didn't care if we didn't look cool. We didn't care if people thought Greg was our friend. The whole thing had been too much for us.

Dean stood there watching us.

"What's Greg talking about?" Dean asked.

It was lucky that Dean was such a stupid ghost. He had no idea what we were up to.

He gave us all hell that day, me and Markie and Greg.

He tipped over Greg's class project which was a whole jarful of frogs. They jumped around everywhere. It had taken

Greg weeks to collect them and he was in tears.

Then Dean locked the science teacher in the cupboard with the frogs, and threw away the key. She was in there all day, crying and shouting, and it was Greg who got the blame.

"We've got to get that ghost to go!" he wailed.

At lunchtime, Dean pushed Markie's head into his plate of food just when he was trying to show Sunna how cool he was. And it's very hard to look good with mashed potatoes all over your face.

Sunna went off laughing with all her friends and Markie wailed, "We've got to get that ghost to go!"

In the boys' toilets Dean locked Big Harry, the biggest boy in the school, in one of the booths, and do you know who got the blame? Me. I was the only other one in there, so who else could have done it? And what did I get in return? Big Harry pushed my head down the toilet and flushed it.

He said it might get rid of the smell.

The smell was everywhere. By the end of the day I had been put in a corner of the classroom, on my own. Not on my own, of course. Dean was there, right beside me. Grinning.

I had only one thought in my head, *We've got to get that ghost to go!*

Chapter 8
Dead Scared

After school the three of us – me, Greg and Markie – went off to the park. Greg said we must go to the place where I first saw Dean. That was where we had to get rid of him.

I say the three of us, but it was really the four of us. Dean was with us all the time.

"Where are we going?" he kept asking.

When he saw we were getting near the park, he started to jump about. "I love going to the park," he said. "Now, where's that stupid Ross and his stray dogs? I hate those animals. I would hate to live in his house."

Just then Ross came round a corner. He had six of his dogs with him. As soon as they saw Dean they began to growl and bark.

"Look!" yelled Dean. "They're dead scared of me! This is great!" And then he got ready to kick those poor dogs again.

The dogs watched him coming. They yelped. They pulled Ross right off his feet. Then they were off, with Dean right after them.

"Come back here!" I yelled to Dean. But he didn't hear me. He was having too much fun.

"Where is he now?" Greg asked.

"Chasing Ross and his dogs. Look!" It *was* funny. You just had to laugh. Ross was being dragged along by the dogs. He was trying to hold them back. And Dean gave Ross a few kicks as he ran past him.

"We can't get rid of Dean if he's not here," yelled Greg. "Get him back!"

We had to wait until Dean and Ross and the dogs had all run right round the park and came up close to us again. It was Markie and me who grabbed Ross and stopped him and his dogs from running past us again.

"Do you want your dogs to stop dragging you round this park every day?" I asked.

Ross nodded.

"Well, tie them to a tree and do just what we do."

We *all* had to work hard to tie up the dogs. They just didn't want to stay. They were going wild.

Dean thought we were trying to help him. "Thanks, boys," he said. "Now I can scare them and they can't even run away."

I felt sorry for the poor dogs. "It won't be for long," I tried to tell them.

"This *will* work, won't it?" Markie asked Greg.

"Of course!" Greg said. Then he added, "Well, I hope it will. Now, do everything I do."

He started chanting this Indian music.

"I don't know what he's up to," Markie said. Greg told him to shut up and join in. So he did. Greg's eyes crossed. All our eyes crossed. Then Greg began to dance.

"Is he sick?" Ross asked.

Greg began to chant again. This time we could hear the words:

"We've got to get that ghost to go!

We've got to get that ghost to go!"

I joined in:

"We've got to get that ghost to go!"

Then Markie joined in too. Only he was singing it as if it was a rap song:

"We've got to get that ghost to go!

We've got to get that ghost to go!

We've got to get that ghost,

We've got to get that ghost,

We've got to get that ghost to go!"

Greg was angry. "This isn't a joke," he said.

But no-one bothered about him. I liked the rap, so I started singing it too. So did Ross.

And soon the beat got to Greg and he started to dance and sing with the rest of us. I don't know what we must have looked like.

Even Dean joined in. He started dancing and singing as well.

"We've got to get that ghost to go!

We've got to get that ghost to go!

We've got to get that …"

All at once, he stopped singing. "Are you trying to get rid of me?" he asked.

I told you he was thick.

But we didn't stop singing, and Dean began to look worried.

"I feel funny," he said.

"It's working!" I shouted. "Keep singing!"

Dean was fading, a little at a time. First his feet and then his legs.

"Hey! Where are my legs?"

By the time he shouted that, he had vanished up to his middle.

He knew he was going and there was
nothing he could do to stop it. But he gave
me a wicked grin.

"You won't get rid of me!"

Then there was only his face left, an angry face. And his voice. An angry voice.

"I'll be back!" Dean warned me.

His words drifted through the air and made me shiver. But the dogs stopped yelping and their tails started to wag.

"He's gone, hasn't he?" Markie yelled.

"He says he'll come back, and I think he will," I said.

Greg nodded. "Yes, I think he will too. But not as a ghost. He'll come back as something else."

"What?" I asked.

Just then the dogs began barking again and pulling at their leads.

"What's the matter with them now?" Markie asked.

Then we saw an ugly cat watching us from the bushes. A skinny, ginger cat. It arched its back, and showed its teeth and spat at the dogs.

Kind Ross picked it up. "Poor little thing," he said, and he tried to stroke it.

The "poor little thing" scratched him as it tried to get away.

I looked at Greg. "You don't think it could be ...?"

Greg bent down over the cat. "You mean ... Dean?"

The cat spat and sprang at him. It sunk its claws into his face and didn't let go. It took all of us to pull its claws free from Greg. Then the cat jumped down and ran off. The dogs were after it in a flash.

"If that cat is Dean," I said, "I don't feel at all sorry for it. Dean was always chasing those dogs. Now they're getting their own back."

Greg had blood all over his face. "It's Dean all right," he said. "It's got one green eye and the other one's blue."

Markie jumped in the air. "We did it!" He jumped on me. "We did it, Duncan!"

I jumped on him too and then we both jumped on Greg. "We did it!"

Ross didn't understand what it was all about but he jumped on the lot of us. "We did it!" he yelled. Then he shook his head. "What *did* we do?"

Chapter 9
Dead Cool

Did things go back to normal after that? No, everything changed.

We had to stay friends with Greg. He'd saved us. And we had said we'd teach him to be cool. But we didn't have to, because when the ginger cat scratched his face it left a great big scar. Now he really does look like Harry Potter, and that makes him dead cool.

Anyway, it's not all that important to be cool now. You see, Dean thought he was cool and there is no way me and Markie want to be like Dean.

Markie and Sunna are always together now, and someone has written:

Markie loves Sunna

in the boys' toilets.

I always had a funny feeling that Markie fancied Sunna. Sunna says she started to like Markie when she saw him with mashed potatoes all over his face.

"But I looked stupid," Markie said.

"I know. But I think I like you that way," she said.

Ross is our friend now too. He waits for us at the park every day. He even comes

with us to the cinema at the weekend.
Funny thing is, he's really good fun. I don't
know why we didn't let him be our friend
before.

He kept the ginger cat. He took it home with him to live with all the other strays. "Well, we've only got dogs," he said, "and I've always wanted a cat."

He's even called the cat Dean. And almost every day I see it being chased by one of Ross's dogs.

Dean always said he would hate to live in Ross's house with all those dogs. Now his nightmare has come true, because that's just what he does.

And me?

Well, I haven't seen another ghost.

Or have I?

Dean looked like a normal boy. He looked as solid as Markie or me. So, how do I know if I've seen another ghost or not?

How do *you* know?

You could meet one in the street and not know it.

Or you could be standing with one at the bus stop.

Or sitting beside one at the cinema.

They could be all around us, and we don't even know it.

There could be a ghost sitting beside you right now.

It makes you think.

Who is Barrington Stoke?

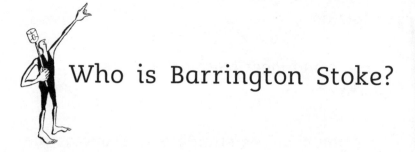

Barrington Stoke went from place to place with his lamp in his hand. Everywhere he went, he told stories to children. Some were happy, some were sad, some were funny and some were scary.

The children always wanted more. When it got dark, they had to go home to bed. They went to look for Barrington Stoke the next day, but he had gone.

The children never forgot the stories. They told them to each other and to their children and their grandchildren. You see, good stories are magic and they can live for ever.

If you loved this story, why don't you read ...

Picking on Percy

by Catherine MacPhail

Has anyone ever picked on you?
Shawn is making Percy's life a misery.
But he is in for a shock when he
discovers to his horror that he is living
Percy's life!

4u2read.ok!

If you loved this story, why don't you read ...

Mad Iris

by Jeremy Strong

Would you like to have an ostrich for a pet? Ross has big problems when one turns up in the school playground. How can he save her from the men in black who want to kill her? And why is Katie stuck in the boys' toilets?

4u2read.ok!